AMAZING MYSTERIES
BIGFOOT

BY MELISSA GISH

CREATIVE EDUCATION • CREATIVE PAPERBACKS

Published by Creative Education and Creative Paperbacks
P.O. Box 227, Mankato, Minnesota 56002
Creative Education and Creative Paperbacks are imprints of
The Creative Company
www.thecreativecompany.us

Design by The Design Lab
Production by Rachel Klimpel
Art direction by Rita Marshall

Photographs by Alamy (Bill Brooks, United Archives GmbH, John Zada), Corbis (Antonino Barbagallo), Dreamstime (Judith Dzierzawa, Sgoodwin4813), Getty Images (Nisian Hughes/Stone, Portland Press Herald), iStockphoto (e71lena, pabradyphoto, ratpack223, THEPALMER), Shutterstock (anatoliy_gleb, Volodymyr Burdiak), Unsplash.com (Barrett Ward, Robert Zunikoff)

Copyright © 2022 Creative Education, Creative Paperbacks
International copyright reserved in all countries. No part of this book may be reproduced in any form without written permission from the publisher.

Library of Congress Cataloging-in-Publication Data
Names: Gish, Melissa, author.
Title: Bigfoot / Melissa Gish.
Series: Amazing mysteries.
Includes bibliographical references and index.
Summary: A basic exploration of the appearance, behaviors, and origins of Bigfoot, the hairy mythological creatures known for their large footprints. Also included is a story from folklore about a woodsman who feeds Bigfoot.

Identifiers:
ISBN 978-1-64026-486-1 (hardcover)
ISBN 978-1-68277-037-5 (pbk)
ISBN 978-1-64000-613-3 (eBook)
This title has been submitted for CIP processing under LCCN 2021937601.

Table of Contents

Ape or Human? 4

Sasquatch 7

Bigfoot Relatives 11

Curious Creatures 12

Tracking Bigfoot 19

Fragmented Film 20

A Bigfoot Story 22

Read More 24

Websites 24

Index 24

Black, brown, or reddish hair covers Bigfoot's body.

Bigfoot is a tall, shaggy creature. It is covered with hair like an **ape**. But it walks upright like a human. Adults are six to nine feet (1.8–2.7 m) tall. Young ones are shorter.

ape an animal in the group that includes gorillas, chimpanzees, orangutans, and gibbons

Bigfoot might eat anything—fruit, flowers, deer, and garbage!

Bigfoot live throughout North America. They are most common in the Pacific Northwest. The Salish people called them *Sasq'ets*. This means "hairy man." Today, Bigfoot is also known as Sasquatch.

Salish a group of American Indian and First Nations peoples of British Columbia, Washington, Oregon, and northern California

People who look for Bigfoot are called trackers.

Bigfoot is named for the large footprints it leaves. Its footprints can be 24 inches (61 cm) long. Bigfoot families live in thick **conifer** forests. They do not wear clothes. Their hair keeps them warm.

conifer a tree that is always green, such as pine and juniper

BIGFOOT

Abominable (uh-BOM-eh-neh-bul) Snowman is another name for Yeti.

Other creatures like Bigfoot are found around the world. The Yeti lives in the Himalayas of Asia. The Yeren of central China has long, red hair. The Australian Yowie's name comes from an **Aboriginal** word meaning "dream spirit."

Aboriginal relating to the Aborigines, the people who first lived in Australia

Bigfoot
live in small family groups. They talk to each other with screams, howls, and whoops. They are curious but shy. They will get near to horses but run away from dogs.

Male Bigfoot are larger than female Bigfoot.

Bigfoot are interested in people.

They like to watch hikers and campers. You can lure a Bigfoot to your campsite with fruit. But it will come only after dark.

Bigfoot have a good sense of smell and eyes that can see best in the dark.

You will know when a Bigfoot has visited your campsite. The creature leaves a terrible smell behind. In Florida, Bigfoot is called Skunk Ape.

Bigfoot might be able to run 30 miles (48.3 km) per hour.

17

BIGFOOT

Many people search for Bigfoot. They report their sightings. The Bigfoot Field Researchers Organization looks for facts about Bigfoot.

More than 3,000 sightings of Bigfoot have been reported.

The first video of a Bigfoot sighting was taken in 1967.

Taking a picture of Bigfoot is hard. Bigfoot may give off **paranormal** energy that affects cameras. Photos are blurry, and video is grainy. No one can explain why no clear images of Bigfoot exist.

paranormal actions that cannot be explained by science

A Bigfoot Story

An old man sold his house in the woods to a young man. He told the new owner, "I have been feeding bears every night. You must do the same." The young man did as he was told. During his first night in the house, the man heard growling. He went outside and shined a flashlight. What he saw shocked him. The previous owner had not been feeding bears. He had been feeding Bigfoot!

Read More

Gish, Ashley. *Bigfoot*. Mankato, Minn.: Creative Education, 2020.

Oachs, Emily Rose. *Bigfoot*. Minneapolis: Bellwether Media, 2019.

Tieck, Sarah. *Bigfoot*. Minneapolis: ABDO, 2016.

Websites

CBC Kids: Have You Ever Spotted a Sasquatch?
https://www.cbc.ca/kidscbc2/the-feed/sasquatch-our-furry-friends
Learn more about Bigfoot's other names.

SoftSchools: Bigfoot Facts
https://softschools.com/facts/general/bigfoot_facts/1195/
Read interesting facts about Bigfoot.

Note: Every effort has been made to ensure that the websites listed above are suitable for children, that they have educational value, and that they contain no inappropriate material. However, because of the nature of the Internet, it is impossible to guarantee that these sites will remain active indefinitely or that their contents will not be altered.

Index

appearance 4, 8
families 8, 12
foods 15
homes 7, 8
names 7, 8, 16
sightings 19, 20
similar beasts 11
sounds 12, 22